South

Words and pictures by

DANIEL DUNCAN

ABRAMS BOOKS FOR YOUNG READERS
NEW YORK

There once was a fisherman
who sailed the seas alone.

One day, a sudden noise led him to discover . . .

. . . a fellow traveler with a broken wing.

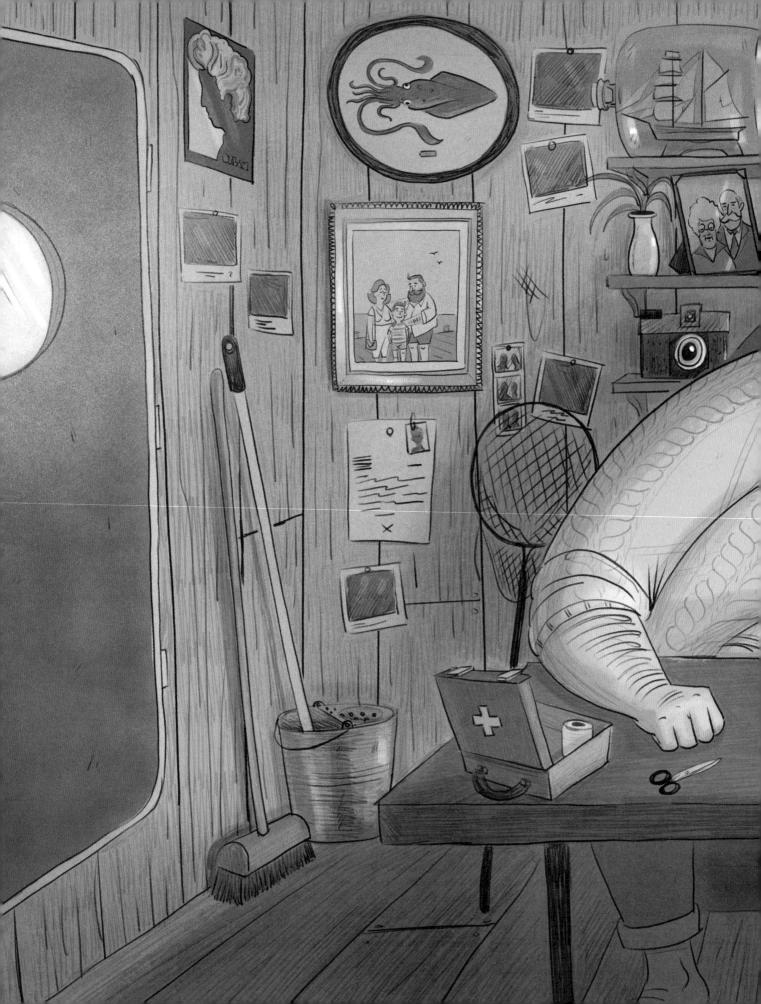

After the bird's wing was bandaged,
all that was left to do was wait.

The fisherman loved how the bird
sang along with his banjo.
The bird loved tasting the fish
caught each day.

But it was getting colder.
And the fisherman knew that his
boat was no home for the bird.

The fisherman
had an idea.

He set sail on a new course: SOUTH

LAND, HO!

With the bird's wing healed, the fisherman knew their journey together had come to an end.

It was time to say good-bye.

The boat felt a little quieter
after the bird had gone . . .

. . . but the fisherman would always remember his friend.

He set sail on a new course:

HOME

Cataloging-in-Publication Data has been applied for and may be
obtained from the Library of Congress.

ISBN: 978-1-4197-2299-8

Text and Illustrations copyright © 2017 Daniel Duncan
Book design by Maria T. Middleton and Chad W. Beckerman

Printed and bound in China
10 9 8 7 6 5 4 3 2 1

Abrams Books for Young Readers are available at special discounts
when purchased in quantity for premiums and promotions as well
as fund-raising or educational use. Special editions can also be created
to specification. For details, contact specialsales@abramsbooks.com
or the address below.

ABRAMS The Art of Books
115 West 18th Street, New York, NY 10011
abramsbooks.com

31192021218720